COVID ARCHIVES

NINE SHADES OF HUMAN EMOTIONS DURING COVID TIMES

DEEPIKA SRIVASTAVA

Made with ♥ on the Notion Press Platform
www.notionpress.com

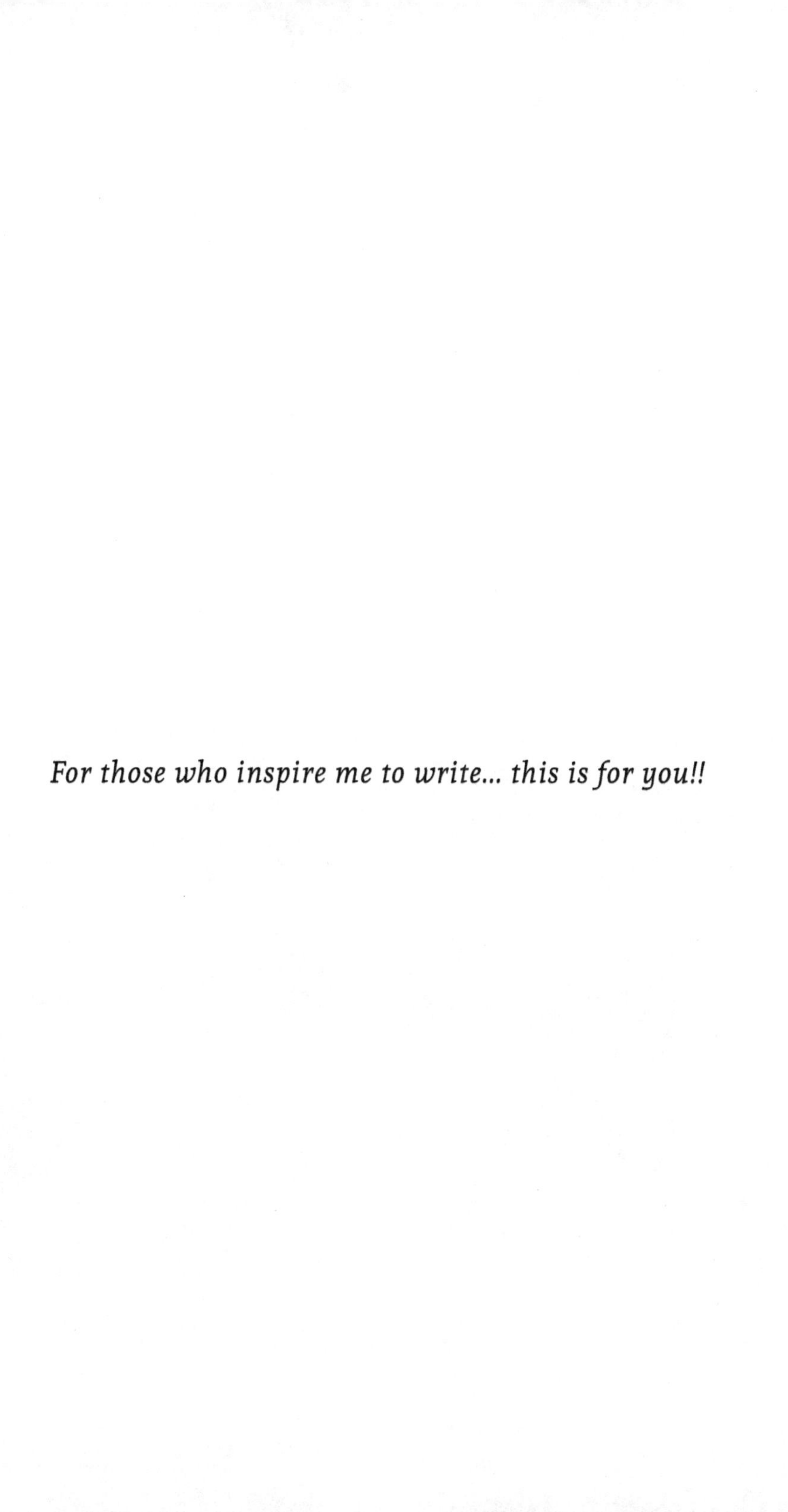

For those who inspire me to write... this is for you!!

Contents

Preface

2019. A virus hits China. The world still unaware, passes it off as another piece of news. Some even read coronavirus as carnivorous in the first go.... Gradually the virus starts making its presence felt as a pandemic. COVID-19 shakes the entire mankind.... Not even a single being left unaffected. The disease...the unseen virus created medical, financial, and emotional emergencies throughout the globe. Everyone has a different story to tell. Here, I have come up with nine such stories weaving every emotion.... some could be relatable, and some fictitious. Nine emotions of love, loss, happiness, sorrow, revenge, hope, courage, surprise, and fear... penned into stories of Covid times.

Foreword

Creating stories about the most crucial times in human history was not a serene and peaceful experience. The idea of knitting nine human emotions into stories of the Covid times has been a present to me by someone cherished and this book is a reciprocation... a gift from me.

These stories are all close to my heart and many times while drafting them... editing them, I had been overwhelmed. Some fiction and some reality are all amalgamated to crave this piece of work.

This book contains the story of my best friend and the trauma of losing her love that she is going through.... Seeing her broken torments me the most. She has always been an inseparable part of me and I can endlessly pen down her in my words. But someday it would be this way, which is heart-wrenching.

This book is for her...

Prologue

Nine shades of human emotions during COVID times.

ONE

A PERFECT LOVE STORY

"Let's go to Goa! It would be fun."

" Not Goa, how about the heaven on earth... Kashmir? The beautiful snowclad mountains. White gold all around us."

" I want to go to the beach, mesmerizing blue waters all around. Sitting for hours on the golden sand. A perfect honeymoon it would be."

" Perfect honeymoon would be cosy Kashmir. Çuddling up together in a blanket... that would be perfect honeymoon, stupid."

This argument knew no end. Until, Radhika got upset and went to still in the balcony.... alone. Rohan can't see her upset and dull. She knew well inside, she was the undefeated queen of all the arguments and this was no different. Smiling silently, at her upcoming victory, Radhika sat on the cane swing pondering why is Rohan taking so much time. The cane swing had its own story. Rohan got it especially designed and personalized for Radhika. He had proposed to her for being his for lifetimes to come, while she was swinging on it in the furniture shop. An absolutely weird and out-of-the-world place to propose to someone. Radhika often used to tell this to Rohan. His reply was, " What if you said no? Then I wouldn't have brought this swing home, na." Rohan and his stupid logic always made Radhika wonder if he still needed to mature.

Talking about seriousness and maturity, Rohan was again no match. He was her best advisor, counselor, and guide. When Radhika's parents didn't agree with her choice of career, he was the one who convinced them about her approach. Today she may not be a leading name in the Footwear Designing industry but she is definitely making her niche in the field. Her father, the most apprehensive one is the proudest man today.

This is how they have been growing and progressing together holding each other's hand. Married a couple of weeks ago, they had a long courtship period of ten years. They met each other for the first time at an interschool competition. Later they went to the same coaching institute. Began as friends, progressed as lovers, and finally settled down as life partners. Their story has been more like a Bollywood masala movie. Rohan comes from an affluent business family. His father offered to invest in Radhika's footwear design but they wanted to start from scratch. However, the offer is always open as his father tells him. Rohan after doing his MBA, joined the family business. The two of them mutually decided not to leave their hometown as their parents needed them. Lucknow may not be a big market for their dreams to grow but thanks to the ever-growing technology, the world has cluttered up in the web. Working online together gives them more time to be close.

"Phew! Where has Rohan disappeared.", Radhika fumingly thought.

" Achcha theek! I will carry you in my arms on the sunkissed beaches of Goa.", Rohan came out of the kitchen holding a bowl of her favorite cheesy Maggi.

" Together with you, beach mountain, or desert, every place is my haven." Rohan bowed in front of his love and kissed her forehead.

Radhika couldn't speak a word but just giggled at her love. Tapping the place next to her she signalled Rohan to sit on the swing. Rohan kept the bowl on the stool next to the swing. He pulled her up sat on the swing and pulled her back on his lap.

"Beautiful us!", Rohan whispered in her ear.

Radhika was smitten under his charm.

It was the first week of March, and Rohan and Radhika had started the preparations for their honeymoon in Goa. Their tickets were for 20th March. Radhika was busy shopping. Rohan wondered why she needed so many clothes and accessories. But he let her do whatever she wanted. Seeing her happy made his heart flutter. They both reflected each other's joy in their entire persona.

Covid 19, an airborne disease was spreading its wings all over the world. The Coronavirus that was infecting the air came from China's Wuhan. No country was left unaffected. India was definitely no exception.

Radhika had read about it on the internet and even the news channels were talking about its seriousness. Rohan became a bit apprehensive about their trip. And before they could actually finalize and cancel their tickets, the airlines cancelled all domestic and international flights.

With heavy hearts, they had no option but to postpone their much-awaited honeymoon.

It didn't take much time for the whole world to come to a standstill. Everything, literally everything, was closed. A nationwide lockdown was implemented.

Rohan was more than happy for now it was just Radhika and him. Nobody to disturb them... No work to be done... Nowhere to go...just they and their home sweet home. This was the most unexpected but always longed-for time that they were going to spend with each other. He tried to uplift Radhika's sullen face.

It was a beautiful vibrant morning, Radhika was still asleep when the sunrays fell on her face and she tried to cover her face. Rohan pulled her closer and she hid her face in his chest. Her lips were on his chest. Rohan could feel the sensation. It was seduction at its height. Radhika sleepily looked up at his face. She made circles on his chest with her finger. Rohan laughed and that encouraged her moves. Her finger was replaced with her tongue and her tongue with her teeth. She moved up and kissed his shoulder. Rohan pulled her up and kissed her lips.

" Good morning, sweetheart!!", He whispered close to her mouth as he again bent over to kiss them.

Radhika was relishing being served by her man. Lazily, she lay there in his arms as he painted his love all over her face. Radhika was in no mood to let him go. She made way for him to go down on her. Rohan worked on her throat...biting her shoulders... His hands caressed her closer to his body. She could feel him over herself. She loved the feel. Together they lay there till noon... caressing and kissing and smooching and loving and teasing each other, when Radhika felt hungry. She got up and prepared their comfort food sandwiches and coffee. Having had their fill, they again cuddled up on the couch. Radhika read a book while Rohan irritated her by pulling her cheeks in between.

With no facility for online food ordering available, they even made lunch and dinner together.

"This is so satisfying and beautiful,na?", Radhika remarked.

"Doing nothing and just being with each other. We would have never had such precious moments even if we had gone to Goa. This is pure bliss!", She continued.

"It's your presence that adds magic to these mundane times. Thanks for being mine.", Before Rohan could finish Radhika hugged him with tears of love and joy in her eyes.

She thought to herself, "He is such an adorably amazing person... I'm blessed to call him mine."

This is how days transform into weeks and weeks into months. Away from the world they found bliss in theirs.

A few days later, Rohan felt uneasy and nauseous. He didn't tell Radhika because he didn't want her to worry. But this uneasiness soon got worse and his temperature rose. Fever in these times, meant panic. Rohan got tensed and worried.
He then called Radhika, "Radhika! I'm not feeling well. A little bit feverish."

Radhika too got worried. Though she consoled him, " Don't worry, I will give you a paracetamol and you rest. You will feel better."

Rohan took the medicine and slept.

Radhika was getting restless. She called up her brother, who was a doctor, and told him about Rohan, " Bhai, Rohan is having fever and I am not able to comprehend anything. What should I do?"

" First and foremost, calm down. If you would behave like this how will Rohan get better? And as a doctor I would suggest, you go in for a RTPCR."

"But we hardly go out anywhere or meet anyone. We always keep our faces covered and use sanitizers almost every time, we come back from the market. Even I go out with him, had he been infected, so would I be..."

" I said calm down and relax, understand it's an easily transmittable virus, so you need to double-check. And conducting a test doesn't mean he is positive. It's just a possibility."

" But....", Radhika tried to speak but her brother made her stop.

" I am sending a medical team and get Rohan's COVID test done. Hopefully the reports would be negative.", He asserted.

Radhika was becoming nervous and petrified. She slightly opened the bedroom door and peeped inside. Rohan was serenely asleep. Watching him, she reminisced how she used to wonder, "Had I been Rohan, I would have been super proud and arrogant for being him. But this man didn't even know what it meant to be proud leave aside arrogance."

Seeing him in deep slumber, she prayed for everything to be fine. Later that day, Rohan's sample was taken for RT-PCR. Rohan kept his cheerful disposition and tried to motivate Radhika. Rohan didn't let Radhika near him. And this was frustrating for Radhika. Her annoyance and nervousness knew no bounds.

They both kept their fingers crossed as they waited for the test results. The result was expected by the evening. Radhika was feeling lost and missing in her own home.

At around six in the evening, her brother called up.

"Hello bhaiya!, All's well na?", Radhika said frantically.

To her horror, the report was positive. Her nightmare came alive. She was in a cold sweat. Now what?

Raghav, her brother, informed her that he was trying to arrange a bed for Rohan at Covid Centre.

This made Radhika colder.

How can she let Rohan go? No she can't and she wouldn't. But the protocol has to be followed.

"What if I want Rohan to isolate himself at home?", She enquired Raghav.

"The protocol says, home quarantine would only be allowed at non-availability of beds at the Covid Centre. And he cannot change the rules.", Raghav answered.

Rohan was in his room resting, when Radhika broke the news to him. At first, he was shocked but one look at Radhika's deprived face made him act stronger.

"Don't you worry, it's all a matter of a fortnight and I will be perfectly fine.", He consoled Radhika.

Raghav's next phone was like a little ray of hope amidst a quantum of darkness.

"We will have to home quarantine Rohan as all Covid Centres in the city are full. I will try my best to arrange a bed at the earliest." " he said not having the slightest idea how overwhelmed Radhika was by this shortage.

Her Rohan would be home at least. She promised Raghav that she would follow his instructions and take proper care of Rohan and herself.

She went to the bedroom and peeped inside Rohan was still asleep. She went to the kitchen and prepared vegetable soup and Rohan's favourite pasta.

Lost in her thoughts and work, she didn't hear Rohan calling her. Rohan called over her mobile phone. Her thoughts were broken by the ring. She realised Rohan must be hungry. She immediately plated the food and arranged it in a tray for Rohan.

She was about to enter the room in her normal sway when Rohan stopped her.

"Stop! You don't come near me. Keep the tray there at the door and I will pick it up."

She followed his instructions and came out.

Her eyes were welled up. She silently cried and tried to eat her food.

It was bedtime, she was sitting outside the room and kept looking at Rohan from a distance. She tried to close her eyes but sleep alluded her. Anxiously, she walked up and down the corridor. The moment she tried to sit, she felt more restless.

And suddenly in the spur of the moment, she went inside the room. Kissed Rohan's forehead and sat quietly next to him and then hugged him tight. She is not going anywhere leaving Rohan alone. It was her room, her bed, and her Rohan. Hugging him tight, she slept next to him. Rohan was under the influence of medicine and didn't feel anything.... but a sense of serendipity when Radhika hugged him. They both slept peacefully. Radhika woke up before Rohan and went to the washroom. She took a shower and was feeling much more relaxed after a sound sleep. Went to the kitchen and started preparing breakfast. Then she took it to his room, and called out Rohan's name. He woke up and said, "I am keeping your breakfast here. Come and take it. Then I will give you the medicines."

Rohan was quite taken aback at her relaxed temperament. He could smell her fragrance all over him.

"You slept here beside me last night?", He asked.

She nodded in guilt.

" But I can explain.,..", she innocently said.

Rohan was annoyed.

"You would have not let me sleep alone, and I know that well, isn't it.!", She added.

"Also I can't sleep without you, so I had no option but to sleep next to you or not sleep at all... for a complete fortnight and that would have been more frightening and unsafe." " she said while looking down at the floor.

Rohan," Then there's no point standing there when you would be doing the same every night. Come inside."

She smiled from ear to ear and sat on the chair next to his bed. Together they had their breakfast.

Rohan started recovering gradually and Radhika fortunately didn't get infected. They kept all negative thoughts at bay. Together they laughed and lived every moment of that quarantine period.

Radhika kept updating Raghav and religiously followed his instructions and guidelines.

One afternoon when Rohan was deep asleep, Radhika came inside and sat on the chair next to him.

Stroking his hair she quipped, "On second thought, Kashmir would be a better experience than Goa...!"

Rohan heard her and smiled, "Wow! All my efforts were negligible and this virus changed your opinion without any...!!"

Radhika kissed his palm, "Anything for you."

TWO
SORROW

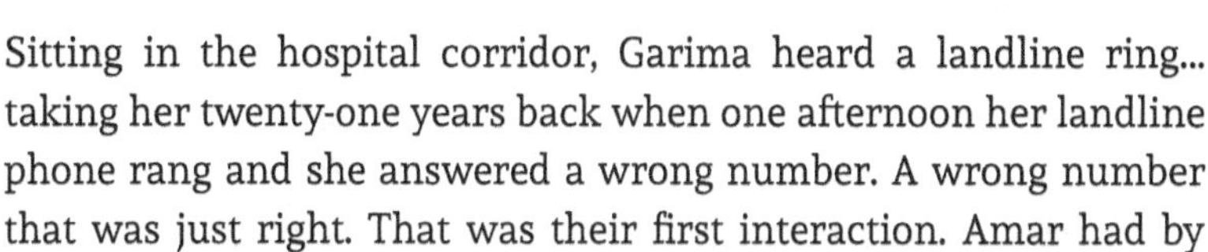

Sitting in the hospital corridor, Garima heard a landline ring... taking her twenty-one years back when one afternoon her landline phone rang and she answered a wrong number. A wrong number that was just right. That was their first interaction. Amar had by mistake dialed the wrong number. Their first conversation lasted a few seconds but a connection stronger was established.

The next day Amar called up again, exactly at the same time. Somehow Garima was also expecting him to call... And when the phone rang, she knew it was him. Some random questions and answers led to deep conversations that lasted hours.

She was lost in the mayhem of those memories when the nurse tapped her on her shoulder.

"The doctor wants to talk to you", she said to Garima.

Garima looked at Amar lying there with an oxygen mask covering his face. How much she wanted to talk to him but it's been days now, since she last heard his voice. Wearily she got up and went to the doctor's chamber.

Maybe, the doctor will tell her to take Amar home as he is recovering well. With this hope, she greeted the doctor with a smile.

"See Garima, I am not going to give false hopes. Amar's condition is deteriorating and there is not much we can do. He is critical."

"Hmmm, that means we have to take extra care and provide him with better medications.", Garima replied.

"We would be shifting him on a ventilator machine and I can't assure you anything.", the doctor said and called the nurse. He instructed her about the further process. While Garima sat there dumbfounded and numb.

Her elder brother and sister waited for her outside. They too didn't have any words to console her.

Post COVID-19 Amar developed a severe lung infection and ever since then, his condition has been going down. Garima had been running from one hospital to another to get her man back. But her efforts were going futile.

(Garima, the most pampered and loved youngest child of a large joint family, has always been strong but seeing her in this situation even more strong makes everyone around her weak. Amar cared for her like a baby and loved her beyond the world. They haven't left each other's side even for a minute in these twenty-one years.)

It's been almost a month since Amar was hospitalized. In these four weeks, Garima had lived those twenty-one years an infinite number of times. She even imagined how she would take care of Amar once he got well.

The situation all over the country was becoming grave. The media was all about COVID-19 and its impact on the lives of the common man. A year ago things were still far better. The death rate wasn't as high as this time. Lockdown came as bliss for most of the families, who enjoyed quality time with each other. For the first time in anyone's remembrance, it was a long unexpected but much-needed holiday for all. Shops, offices, schools, restaurants, trains, and even flights were shut down for public good. Roads wore a deserted look with only policemen strolling down the streets to keep a check on the notorious elements of the society. People were getting infected but still they were recovering. Those who died of COVID-19 were people who were acquaintances of the acquaintances. Everyone expected this phase to pass away soon and life would return to normal. Nobody expected that the virus would ever be completely gone. And it would become deadlier than the first outbreak.

Garima, too was working from home and took care of the minutest aspect of safety all by herself. Taking care of her parents and mother-in-law. Being extremely particular about Amar's lifestyle. She made it a point that no one was leaving the house until and unless it was an emergency. For everything else, she made arrangements at home. From fresh fruits and vegetables to all the other essential items, everything was either delivered at the doorsteps or it was she who went out to purchase them. House help was provided with masks and sanitizers. She did it all. Building a small fort of safety for her family.

And still... this happened.

In the wee hours of the day, Garima received a phone call from the hospital, and the unexpected happened. Amar couldn't cope with the artificial life support system which left Garima shattered and broken forever.

[23:53, 7/11/2023] Deepika Srivastava Gupta: There was no chaos, no peace, no pain, no relief. All she could feel was a vacuum that was sucking her towards it. She wanted to cry out loud but she couldn't even put in her slightest effort. Numb. Silent. She felt no pain... No anxiety. It wasn't disturbing at all. Her world was silent all of a sudden. All she could feel was an excruciating ache in her heart. As if it was being pierced by a sharp-edged knife. But she wanted it more.

She couldn't even gather enough courage to see Amar for one last time. In this flow, she realized if she didn't see now, she would never see him again. Never again. Her heart stopped with a thud and she for the first time felt the pain. Her shadow left her.

He was her reflection, standing beside her in all circumstances. They had a love marriage after seven years of dating. Their relationship was nothing less than a roller coaster ride with more downs than ups. But nothing could deter them from being together.

Amar had introduced Garima to his mom and Masi. They were quite warm and welcoming. Garima too became a part of their small close-knit family. Adapting to an entirely different culture and household was another hurdle that she crossed efficiently and effortlessly. Yes, effortlessly it seems to us, but she put in all of herself to maintain the equilibrium. Garima and Amar both being the only children of their parents, had to manage both families. But they never failed anyone. Though they too had their conflicts, together they overcame all. Every sorrow had to pass off when they were faced it holding hands... fighting against the odds and even with each other.

This sorrow was there to stay for every living moment of her life. Seeing Amar's lifeless body made her lifeless. She realized he was never going to hold her hands again. This never made her more numb....

Life is never going to be the same again. The bubbly chirpy girl full of life, would now be hiding her unending pain with a fake smile.

Months later, even today she wakes up in the middle of the night, feeling lost. All she could ask for was Amar....

THREE
SURPRISE

Her joy knew no bounds, when finally Rachna's father-in-law agreed to her taking up a job. She felt at the top of the world. She was happy beyond limits...

She was arranging her home, that she had so meticulously crafted. Every nook and corner had her impression. She filled the rooms with the colors of her dreams. A magnificent dancing peacock that adorned the plain white drawing wall, was symbolic of her aspirations that were as vivid and colorful as the peacock. The artifacts on the opposite shelf were all hand-picked. As a newlywed, some fifteen years ago, Rachna made this house a dream home for its souls. You cannot miss out on the intricacies with which she had decorated it. A dreamer she was...and her dreams well reflected in her soulful house...

Today everything looked inviting and alluring, as if those lifeless showpieces were rejoiced at her ecstasy....as if they all shared her dreams with her.

Her father-in-law, a retired government clerk was an inexorable and hard-headed person. Convincing him was a herculean task. He came from an orthodox family and had a submissive wife. His wife, Rachna's mother-in-law, was a simple but strong lady. She supported her husband and his family in all ups and downs. She was the rock who kept the family firm. However, she passed away a few years before Rachna's wedding. Sometimes Rachna missed having her around. She wondered if had she been there, maybe she could speak her heart out. She wanted to be like her mother-in-law but not at the cost of her dreams.

Her inner urge to prove herself kept nagging her to explore the world. Gifted with a euphonic voice, she worked as an RJ before getting married fifteen years ago to a banker, Rahul. She had to compromise on her career to complete her home and family. But there was always an incompleteness that she felt. She too had dreams to fulfill. She got busy in the household but was determined to realize her dreams someday.

Rahul was the most beautiful happening of her life. Simple yet strong like his mother, he was the support system of the family and above all Rachna's. Rahul and Rachna had an arranged marriage, where they hardly met each other before the wedding. Rahul was posted in another city. Getting to know her man through phone calls and Skype video calls, was a dicey situation. As for Rahul, he heard her beautiful voice every morning on the radio. Over the calls Rahul used to tease her, "I'm getting accustomed to listening to your voice every morning."

Rahul had already told her that taking up a job would be difficult for her. She knew the cons but Rahul's love and affection made up for it all over the years.

Life was not a fairytale. But together they outlived all problems. Sitting on the couch, Rachna reminisced about the difficult time of her pregnancy. Those nine months were like an eternity. Her doctor advised her to complete bedrest as the child's growth was not at its pace. She locked all her aspirations in a closet and gave herself entirely to her daughter. Taking care of her even before she was born. Days and nights became one. Her daughter was normal but lagged behind the kids of her age. The regular comparisons of relatives and friends made her apprehensive. Rahul was the only one who understood Rachna's apprehensions. He used to tell her, " It's not the same for all kids. Every child progresses as per his stamina. And it's perfectly all right if our daughter was taking a little more time."

She used to tell stories to her daughter and sing lullabies to her. Rahul used to watch Rachna putting in all her efforts to raise their child. He used to feel sad that because of all these pressures Rachna couldn't pursue her dreams. But he was sure that someday, she would get her due...

And finally, that someday was here. Her daughter was grown up and could manage herself. Household responsibilities have also been synchronized over a long period. Rahul had assured her that he would talk to his father regarding Rachna's passion once the time was right. True to his words, he convinced his father after a lot of turmoil. It was the toughest nut to crack.

Rachna used to record small audio clips, sometimes while reading a book, sometimes snippets of poems that she taught her daughter. Since Rachna desperately wanted to do this for herself. She started working on the outlines without anybody's knowledge. Drafted an impressive resume, made a collection of her audio clips, and even arranged records of her shows as an RJ.

She knew she had no time to waste. She mailed her credentials to a few radio channels. And finally got selected for an audition by one of the newly launched radio channels.

The interview cum audition was scheduled for the next week. When she told Rahul about it. He was more shocked than surprised and also apprehensive about his father. He didn't want to upset anyone of the two. However, he knew that he would have to keep his promise to Rachna. He put in all his efforts to persuade his stubborn-fashioned father. Ultimately, he gave up on his obstinacy, though reluctantly at the beginning. He was annoyed and doubtful as to how the house be managed without a woman. Rahul tried his best and made him understand that even Rachna's dreams are valuable and they should not overlook the efforts that she has made as an awesome daughter-in-law, loving and caring mother, and a supportive wife. It was time now to give her what she deserved... and let her fulfill her dreams.

Sometimes, destiny plays awful jokes. Amidst all this, there in the background, all over the world, Coronavirus was spreading its wings. WHO declared it a pandemic. No country or city was left unaffected. The government of India declared all schools and colleges to be closed till the situation isn't under control. Rachna's scheduled audition also got postponed... till when? Nobody knew. The situation was becoming grave all over the country.

Rachna lost all her dreams to the pandemic. She knew well, that for the safety of her daughter, it was important she stayed home and attended online classes. For her dreams, they took a backseat again.

Days... Weeks and months, life had come to a standstill for all. Her husband too worked from home. Rachna got engrossed in her household chores again but the ache in her heart was still there. Rahul could see that in her eyes. He just wanted to do something for her. He could make out her sadness.

One evening Rachna got a call from a YouTube channel's content creator, that they were looking for a fresh voice for the voiceovers of the channel's content. They sent Rachna a script and asked her to record it in her voice and send it over WhatsApp.

Rachna pinched herself and couldn't believe her stars. She gave her best performance and secured the job. Now she could easily realize her dreams without compromising on her family's needs.

(Rahul, her husband, played the catalyst. He shared Rachna's distress with a friend who was a YouTuber. He came up with this brilliant proposal as he too wanted to start another channel but his plans went array because of the pandemic. Both of them found a solution to their despair.)

Rachna found her miracle!!

FOUR
LOSS

Dear Diary,

Today as I turn 16, I want to share the most beautiful story I have heard. I so desperately wish I could have experienced it in full instead of having heard it in tits and bits...with welled-up eyes.

Years 2020 and 2021, were two dreadful years in the history of mankind. Destiny brought me into this world in the latter. I still don't understand whether I should be happy about being born on that day that year or regret that day that year as the worst of my life. I lost what I could never find again... Every single day I lived with this feeling of loss...a forever and irreparable one. I wish I could just get one moment of happiness on my birthday every year but it's doomed to never happen. The day I was born I lost my father to Covid 19. The irony being he was able to get the news of my birth but I could never feel the warmth of his words.

My mom keeps telling me stories of my dad. She adorns a brave smile every time but I can feel that lump in my throat. When I was small, I never missed my dad because never knew he ever existed. My grandfather, my Baba, was the only male I knew as an infant. Gradually as I started to know relations, I realized I didn't have a father around... or maybe he was there in every album we had at home, in pen drives, mobile phone gallery, and in his pictures that adorned the walls of our home. He was seen with friends, baba and Dadi, with my mom (there are countless of them), with so many people he shares a picture. But none with me, this started bothering me when I learned to understand things. He was a constant figure in our house he is still one. However, for me he is a stranger I am so familiar with. He resembles me in appearance or maybe as everyone else says, I resemble him. My Dadi says I even talk like him... am patient like him... Mom always sees him in me. But I could never feel it.... It is my forever loss!

It was in 2010, that my dad married my mom. They had an arranged marriage. My Baba was my mom's father's friend. And he always wanted to have my mom as his daughter-in-law. Dad never questioned his decisions. And Baba tells this so proudly even today. Though I am never pushed to follow his decisions... I feel he is too broken inside to feel confident outside. Dad was his pride...his strength.

Dear Diary, you know what disturbs me the most is that why didn't they hate me, when I was born on the day dad passed away! The very thought, what if they did, gives me shivers down the spine. And I shut my eyes and control my fear following through my eyes.

Mom tells me that I was Dad's precious dream after all I was conceived ten years after their wedding. Mom reminisces about that moment as if it was just a moment ago. The doctor had called my father to collect my mom's blood test report. Dad was so nervous that he didn't take Mom along. He went alone. They had been trying for a baby for years but every time it was just disappointment. That day too, Dad was expecting a similar situation.

The doctor, handed my dad a box of chocolates instead of the report this time. Dad was not sure what was happening. He looked haphazardly at the doctor. "Open the box and see what's inside it.", said the doctor.

My father opened the box with trembling hands and butterflies in his stomach. There between the chocolates was a paper with the words...' Positive Pregnancy Test'. My father's joy knew no bounds. He couldn't even utter a thank you to the doctor. Instead just rushed out of the clinic, straight to his car heading home. Mom was restlessly waiting for him to come back. Mom still blushes while telling me how my elated dad hugged her tight at the doorstep with everyone around watching them astonished. He whispered in my mom's ear..." it's positive... We shall live our dream together now." Mom almost fainted listening to his words. He lifted her and made her sit on the couch next to Dadi. And then kissed Dadi's hand as he handed over the report to Baba. My grandparents couldn't control their emotions and danced at the news. I must have felt their joy inside mom's womb but regret not having a superb memory to remember it. At least I would have had something I could relate to with my dad. Mom was two months pregnant at that time. Dad and Baba both wanted me to be a baby girl. Their wish did come true...

The eight months, were only about happiness and joy in abundance, Mom recalls. Dad took care of her like a baby. My grandparents were always affectionate towards her...even when the relatives taunted mom for not being able to conceive after so many years of marriage, they chided them, " Baby will happen whenever it would be destined but first and foremost she is our daughter." They stand by their words to date.

Amidst all this, another mayhem had overcast the world during those months, a pandemic COVID-19 19 had spread like fire all across the world. Not even a single person was left unaffected. Not just on the health front but economically too everyone suffered. Our family was no exception. Dad's salary was cut down to half and now he had to manage all in that meager amount. Despite this increasing burden he used to motivate Mom saying, "I'm there and shall manage all. I have enough savings to cover it up all. The only thing you need to worry about is our baby. She should always be blessed and happy."

Mom tells me that those times were so scary, a lockdown was imposed all around the world and people were petrified of leaving their homes. Even neighbors avoided each other. The news channels were broadcasting pandemic news 24 by 7 creating a sense of horror and dismay. Social media was full of the aftermath of the disease. People were dying not in few but in large numbers. My family was following every possible protocol to avoid the disease. But when

destiny has something else lined up, we are just puppets performing to its whims. Dad who was the only person who left the house whenever needed, got infected with coronavirus. One morning he woke up sick and started developing the symptoms gradually. He called up the Covid Helpline to get a test done. He immediately isolated himself. That second wave of Covid 19 was far more dangerous than the first. Breathing problems, lung infection, and then multiple organ failure followed. Dad tested COVID-19 positive. One more report that had the word positive, but this time it was desperation instead of joy. Dad's condition started worsening within a few days. He was admitted to the ICU. Mom couldn't meet him fearing that she might catch the infection, which in turn would affect me. It was the second week of May, mom had completed her third trimester. Dad was still in the ICU. His lungs were not functioning properly. Every time, he spoke to Baba on the phone, he only pleaded with him," Don't waste this hard-earned savings of our family on me. They are for my daughter. Please... I beg you!"
My grandfather was a strong man because he had my father by his side but dad's condition was making his confidence deter. Dadi prayed day and night for Dad and me... Had she just prayed for Dad, God wouldn't have had a choice. Maybe they would have been happier without me. Mom didn't know what to do, she had to live for me but couldn't live without Dad too. How bravely, she chose me.

On 14th May 2021, Mom felt uneasy and was in labor. Fear and apprehensions got worse, as her water bag got ruptured and she had to undergo a cesarean operation. Within an hour I opened my eyes to this world...only to lose my world's biggest support. Baba immediately called up Dad to give him this happy news. That was the last he smiled. He was just waiting for me to arrive.

Within a few minutes, baba received a call,

" Sorry to inform you sir, but your Raghav is not responding and there are no chances of his survival. All he has is a few last minutes." Baba was sweating profusely and sat on the bench outside my mom's room. He collected himself and headed to the ICU to see Dad for the last time. He called up Dadi to stop her prayers now. Her

Raghav is now back with them but this time as their Raghavi, that's what they christened me. Raghav's reflection Raghavi.

Mom was in deep slumber when she felt Dad's presence around her. She understood her Raghav had gone away handing her his most cherished dream. Now she will have to live without him and for me.

Growing up, I missed Dad every minute. Seeing my friends with their dads made me crave more of his affection. They were all quite generous towards me. And always treated me with special attention. But had Dad been there, I would have had all his love and affection. I desperately wish I could feel that love.... Mom says, Dad would have pampered me and I would have been a spoilt brat. But dear Diary, I just wish it all for one day, at least.

Love you, Dad... My glittering star, the shiniest that decorates the sky.

Raghavi

FIVE

PEACE

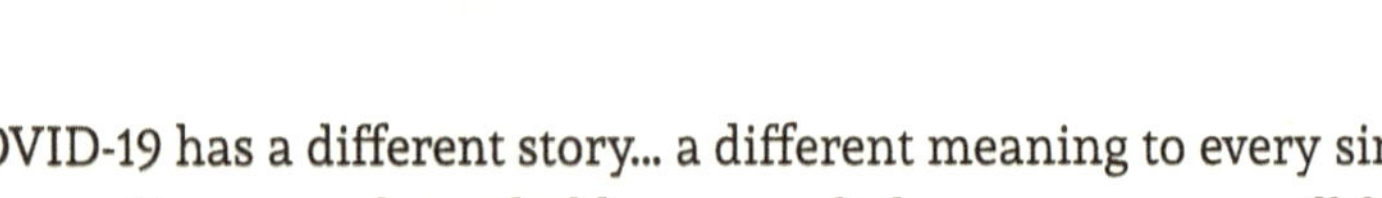

COVID-19 has a different story... a different meaning to every single person. Enter any household, any workplace... everyone will have a different experience to share. Though all were affected by one common cause, some suffered it, some outlived it, many succumbed to it and many more found peace within it.

The loss humankind faces is inevitable. The dark shadows are here to loom over us for lifetimes to come.

This is a story about a footballer by force and a painter by passion. Vihaan.

As a young student in class eight, his father, who was a sportsperson himself, wanted him to undertake any sport as a passion and later on as a profession. Vihaan however had a creative inclination. He was wonderful with colors and his brushes danced to his tunes. Creative people are too sensitive at heart and find hurting others an offense. So was the case with Vihaan. He was too apprehensive to speak out his heart. He feared his father's reaction. He was petrified of his anger. He has some dark memories of his temper, which lay buried deep in his heart. All he wanted was to keep his father's temper normal, if not make him happy.

Vihaan had so much pain inside him and to suppress that agony, he chose to be a boxer. Maybe physical pains would eradicate the pain of his heart. But sometimes what we suffer within is much more excruciating than the wounds visible to the naked eye...

Blankly staring at the ceiling fan at the COVID center, he reminisced every single moment of growing up. His mother's plight and her succumbing to his father's ill temper one night. She was the only person who made him feel loved and wanted. Losing her made Vihaan immune to all pains and miseries. Boxing was not a sport for him, it was a way to vent out the frustration he felt within himself. Not being understood by the world is acceptable but not being able to understand by one's father fills you with bitterness.

These disturbing thoughts never left his mind and the scars on his soul never healed. Every time he was in the ring, either practicing or having a match, his father's actions and words kept ringing in his ears and he became more aggressive towards his opponent. During one such match, he was uncontrollable and hit his opponent so hard that he was comatose for almost a month. Vihaan was debarred from the ring by the Boxing Association. That was the last bout of his aggressiveness. After that Vihaan went into severe depression and was sent to a rehabilitation centre.

He was in the center for some time when Covid 19, started spreading all over the world. The centre was also shut down during the lockdown and Vihaan was sent home. Vihaan despised living there after his mother's death. He had spent his school and college years at hostels. He never went home for vacation. He either stayed back at the hostel or went on lonely solo trips, he hardly had any friends, just a few acquaintances. He kept bare minimum contact with his father. As for his father, he never tried to understand what was going on inside his only child's mind. The thoughts that were churning inside Vihaan were taking him to a desolate world. As a father, he boasted of his son's success as a boxer.

Coming back home was like entering Pandora's box, a box he was scared to even touch leaving aside opening...but this time he had to enter it all alone. At home, he was not welcomed by his father, who was annoyed at his being debarred from the boxing ring. And he didn't even for once try to hide his resentment. Vihaan's frustration knew no bounds. He spent sleepless nights sitting in his mother's room. He couldn't speak a word to his father. He was petrified of his anger... more now.

It was just like living a lifeless life. Getting up in the morning preparing morning tea and breakfast for his father, which they ate mostly in silence. Then spend some time in the garden and then again preparing lunch. Evenings were dull and monotonous, with the only sound of television going on in the background. Then again dinner and a long sleepless night... This became Vihaan's ritual that he followed every day.

One evening, when his father came back from his evening walk. He felt dizzy and tired. He told Vihaan that he won't have anything and would rather go and sleep. Vihaan nodded without even asking why!

The next morning, his father was down with a high temperature. Vihaan gave him medications at home, a cold compress, herbal tea, and everything he could find on the internet. But there was no respite. His condition started worsening. Unwillingly, Vihaan called up the Covid Helpline and arranged for his father's Covid test. The team came in an hour and both, the father and the son underwent a Covid test. The reports were positive and they both were sent to Covid Care Centre. Vihaan's father being critical was admitted to the ICU while Vihaan was taken to another room. In all this haste, Vihaan forgot to bring his mobile phone.

Staring at the roof, he recalled his whole life in a jiffy. And also that he had nothing to do in this room except stare here and there as even his phone wasn't with him.

He tried to calm his mind and relax. In his pursuit of calmness, he heard some strange noise. Someone knocking! He looked from the keyhole of the door but no one was at the doorstep. Again he heard someone knocking but not on the door. It was the wall adjacent to his bed that was being knocked. He tried to listen attentively. Heard a voice...

" Is someone there?", a female voice asked from the other side of the wall.

"Yes! Who is there?", Vihaan answered feeling weird that he was talking to a wall.

"Hi, I'm Ritu, a Covid patient in your adjacent room. I was getting bored alone in this monotonous room, so thought let's try something absurd like knocking on the wall."

"That's fine. Even I am alone in this room and was wondering what to do here all alone.", Vihaan replied.

Something was intriguing about Ritu's voice. He was feeling captivated. He brushed off these thoughts, thinking that he was alone that's why he is feeling so.

" You there! ", Ritu enquired.

"Hmm...", Vihaan nodded.

Ritu started talking about the food that they got at the center. She complained about how bland and tasteless it was. She was full of vibrance and joy. Vihaan was getting more and more inclined and engrossed in her. Ritu kept talking nonstop. And Vihaan was recording her words in his mind. Every word she uttered made its way to his heart... mesmerizing him.

He just replied in a yes...no or maybe.

They had been talking through the wall for almost half an hour now, when Ritu asked him, "What do you do?"

Vihaan's impromptu reply, "I'm a painter." For ages, he had not touched the color palette or held a brush. All he knew was boxing and the ring, so why couldn't he tell Ritu that he was a boxer? Did he lie to her? He questioned himself rhetorically...

"Wow! That's so awesome... I love colors...all of them. Colors add so much beauty to this mundane world. Imagine, a black-white world couldn't have survived. Will you paint for me?"

Vihaan nodded apprehensively, " Definitely once we get out of these enclosed cages... I will paint for you."

He was committing to a stranger, he started talking half an hour ago. This perplexed him.

" No I want you to paint here only, I will narrate you the descriptions and you will bring my words to life through your brushes and colors."

Vihaan loved the way she authoritatively said no to him. He fell in love with her orders.

Ritu interrupted his thoughts," Time to sleep... You also sleep now. Good night."

"Good night, Ritu." Vihaan wanted to add see you soon but couldn't muster the courage.

For the first time after his mother's death, he slept peacefully tonight. No disturbing thoughts or nightmares.

" Good morning, Vihaan.", Ritu woke him up.

Vihaan felt like being in a reverie.

" Good morning", he stumbled with words.

"Go and check if there is something outside your door.", Ritu told him.

He opened the door and found a lot of packets and a wooden canvas stand. He brought all the packets inside carefully. One was big and heavy. Then he lifted the stand and placed it near the talking wall. He opened the packets, there were colors, brushes, and palettes. The bigger packet had canvases. He was astonished to see all these things. He gently touched the colors and brushes. He felt a strange quiver down his spine.

" So now my painter is all set to color my world.", Ritu said in her vibrant tone.

My painter...my world!!

Vihaan desperately wanted to tell her,' Yes forever your painter will keep adding colours of your choice to your world.'

Instead, he asked her," How did you arrange all these things overnight?"

Ritu replied, " Very simple, I asked our attendant to get me all the stuff."

" He acted that they are not allowed to go out and get things for patients but money can do wonders." " she laughed childishly.

Vihaan even loved that.

" Now you better get to work. But wait, first have your breakfast and get ready, I'm not letting you go till it's lunchtime. So have a full diet then we can begin." Ritu ordered him again.

" As you say, madam!", Vihaan agreed.

Vihaan meticulously arranged everything, the white plain canvas on the stand, brushes, and colors with the palette beside it. He was all set to add colors to Ritu's words. However, he was a bit nervous and hesitant, about will he be able to paint and color. It's been ages since he lost touch with his passion...

Amidst, these thoughts, Ritu knocked on the wall, "Ready? Shall we begin?"

"Yeah, all set...", Vihaan replied still in dilemma.

" Have you ever wondered how beautifully nature loves?
It opens up its arms to the dark wandering clouds,
The clouds are full of mystical and rejuvenating love.
The vast sky shrinks and lets the clouds cover it up all.
The young old trees sway to meet their long-distance love.
Rivers and oceans all set out to quench their thirst for love.
The parched fields look up to these clouds to transform them into fertile croplands.
Nature bows and expresses its love
As clouds downpour their affection and fill the hearts of all the creations.
How selflessly the clouds love and give up on their existence.
And how nature bears the tormenting and scorching sun to give rebirth to these clouds.
A love story that never ends...", Ritu recited these words magically and Vihaan's brushes and colors worked as if they were spellbound by her charm.

This continued for hours at a stretch. They talked about life, its complexities, and serenity. Vihaan opened up about his pain to Ritu. He told her about his parents, his boxing days, and all the depression and aftermath.

Ritu was all ears for him. She didn't say anything... no suggestions...no advice. As an intrigued audience she kept listening to his words.

Vihaan felt lighter and at peace.

They followed this routine religiously for the next few days. Until it was time for their RTPCR again. Vihaan had recovered but still had to follow the protocol of fourteen days of quarantine. He was more or less happy as he would be able to spend a couple of days more with Ritu.

Ritu's reports were still positive and her condition wasn't improving. That day she was so exhausted that she couldn't give words to Vihaan's colours. Though she didn't tell Vihaan much about her health. She simply told him," Have a sore throat and a headache today, so you do the paint and describe it to me."

Vihaan got worried, "You are fine na, I think you should talk to the doctor. Should I call him?"

" No, no I am fine... feeling a bit uneasy. You please do as I wish."

Vihaan nodded obediently.

That night Ritu slept early. She was too tired.

Vihaan too tried to sleep but was worried about her. Eventually, he slept too. While in deep slumber, he felt someone sitting next to him stroking his hair... He tried to open his eyes but couldn't. He heard Ritu's voice, " You know Vihaan life is a beautiful journey. However, we don't always get what we want because God has other plans for us. Whatever we go through makes us a better person and we should in return fill this world with vibrant colours and make it beautiful for others. You can do that with your passion. Add life to those who live a lifeless life like your father. Maybe he never got to see the world as he should have. Start from here, give meaning to those meaningless lives, and this way you will live a life worth living. Don't think of the pain of loss, imagine the solace and peace it gifted you with. And you know what I love you!"

Vihaan smiled in his sleep as he hugged his pillow.

The next morning he woke up to lots of noise. Those sounds were from Ritu's room. He wasn't able to comprehend what was happening. But this was making him restless. His heart was thumping louder than usual. He peeped outside his room and called the attendant to ask what was all this chaos about.

"The Covid patient next to your room, passed away last night."

Vihaan felt numb. " You mean Ritu, the girl next door?"

" Yes, that blind girl Ritu. Poor girl had already been through so much in her life. She had lost her eyes to an acid attack by some roadside hooligans. Finally she found peace.", the attendant added.

Vihaan sat down on the floor with a thud. He was sweating profusely. His only ray of hope was gone. He would again be forced back into that darkness. Life has always been cruel to him. All these disturbing thoughts were making their way to his mind when all of a sudden, he saw the first painting he painted for Ritu. He could see Ritu smiling and recalled his last night's dream. It wasn't a dream, it was Ritu, who had visited him. In a flash, he felt peaceful again. Ritu had filled him with so much of herself that now he didn't feel disturbed. He stood up and went near his paintings for her. Touched each one and there was a serenity and calmness he had never experienced ever before.

Ritu, his forever season of love...

SIX
REVENGE

Ever since the outbreak of Covid 19, the world has applauded the frontline workers. They have been showered with praise and gratitude. Our heads are bowed for their relentless efforts and undeterred support. Being human and holding hands with people suffering from one of the most frightening diseases in the history of mankind is not an easy thing to do. In times, when even the closest of kins had to keep themselves away from one another, these frontline workers were God-sent angels.

We talk about everyone who was there fighting the unseen foe. But how often do we talk about those who became the last companions of those who passed away all alone? The frontline workers who lit the pyres of countless strangers. The trauma they must have gone through. Everybody must have reminded them of their people back home.

With meager wages, they are the ones nobody ever thought of. While standing by the pyres of unknown faces, they had to face society's stigma. People avoided them... dreaded them...

The human connection of pain and suffering that kept people close was even broken by this disease. Nobody wants to take the risk as they have family back at home. But what about the families of those who are at risk every moment? Nobody thinks!

Ten pyres were burning in front of me. But only nine of them were dead bodies. The tenth one that burnt that night was my revenge on society. I wanted the world to feel what being burnt alive felt like...

I screamed and wanted my heart to rip apart. Sitting all alone at the cremation ground with pyres all around me, some were still burning and some had burnt out. The rising crimson yellow flames, the smoke of the wood, and the pungent smell of burning human flesh were negligible, and hardly cared about the scene. My mind was revolving around that one body... I burnt alive.

I don't need anybody's validation, I fear no God and I don't bother about society's judgment and verdict. The gleaming water of the river and the serene haunting silence of the place were in perfect contrast as were the high rising hot flames and my heart cold and stone.

I am Rambabu and I have been driving the hearse vehicle for almost ten years now. I work for a government hospital in a big city. Coming from a small neighborhood village, I took this job so to provide for the education of my only sister and family, Radha. At the young of twenty, I too had dreams of having a career in a big city. So I left the village and came here along with my friends. Being immature and new to city life, we had no idea where to begin from. With the little savings we had, we first rented a room. It was a small cubicle with a shared washroom and no kitchen. And we were five. While lying in our open lush green fields we used to look at the stars and dream of them. Reality struck when we were confined to this little cubicle with limited air to breathe, that stars were beyond our reach. We strived hard to keep our spirits high but it was tough. Two of my friends couldn't cope with this way of living and went back to the village. I was not ready to give up, I had to survive and live through this for Radha. She was only ten when I left her at the village and settled here. I started working day and night. I learned to drive so that someday I could buy a taxi for myself and be my own master but that was still a distant dream...
Months passed by and I worked as a taxi driver for wages. I used to save money for Radha's education, for a house here, and at last for my taxi. I said na it was all a distant dream.

One day, a friend of mine found vacancies for a hearse vehicle at the government hospital in a newspaper. It wasn't a paying job but at least it was permanent. We applied and to thank our stars, we even got selected for the job. The very first day of the job was scary and frightening. Going to the mortuary made me shiver. Seeing the dead bodies I almost fainted. And when I regained my senses I saw my colleagues laughing at me and mocked by calling me fragile. One of the senior members of the group, who was the night guard at the mortuary, advised me to have a peg or two of the country-made liquor.

Gradually I composed myself and started my job but not without the help of this newly found addiction. The liquor made my senses numb and I carried the corpses as loads, mechanically.

In a couple of years, I rented my room in a slum. It was not a proper room, it had a thatched roof and resembled more of a hut. But since I had to bring Radha here for good education I needed a separate place.

Radha was a simple girl who could adjust to any situation. She never wanted me to leave our village home and settle here in the city but for my sake, she adjusted. When I brought her to live with me here, she was elated. Having lost our parents to an accident we were each other's constant support. My Bittu, as I called Radha lovingly, was ten years younger than me but she was my guiding star. Every time I found myself lost and restless, I just had to think of her shyly smiling and hiding herself behind anything and anyone familiar. I dreamt of her adorning that white doctor's coat. Though I never told her about my dream. I wanted her to dream for herself and build her world. I wish she could... how desperately I wish she could....!

Bittu had her magic. She could convert the mundane into extraordinary. That's what she did to that hut I rented for her. I always felt guilty about not being able to provide a proper home for my sister. However, she was just happy. Never did she ever complain about the lack of amenities in the house. People were reluctant to rent out the house to someone who drove a hearse vehicle. But that was my job and I respected it.

Bittu always insisted on me getting married but I told her that I would marry only once I was able to provide well for her.

Years passed off! We brother and sister duo were happy in not so a not-so-satisfying world. Radha studied hard and excelled in almost all the subjects. She even managed the house efficiently. I told you that she was magic.

The year 2020 was the beginning of our nightmare. Covid 19 had started spreading all over the country. I started spending more time at the mortuary and crematorium. The situation at the hospital was threatening and frightening. People were getting infected, admitted to the hospital, and dying. This was becoming a routine. Very few patients recovered and went back home. The mortuary was full-bodied bodied wrapped up in black polythene bags. We as the frontline workers had to follow the protocol and keep ourselves covered with a PPE kit. These kits were suffocating and hot. But there was no way out. The scene at the cremation ground was even more nerve-wracking. Pyres burning...burnt and waiting to be burnt all around.

I stopped going home even at night as the landlord had warned that if anyone got infected in the area, it would be because of me. He wanted us to vacate the house but I requested him to let Radha stay. I promised him I wouldn't go home till everything was normal.

On that fateful night, Radha came to the hospital to visit me. She was worried about me. I scolded her for coming there. And those were my last words to my little Bittu face-to-face. Last I saw my sister.

At the hospital, she got infected with the coronavirus, or as everybody said. As front liners, we had regular RT-PCR tests done and I tested negative every time.

Radha went home and within a week, she started showing symptoms of COVID-19. She called me up and told me that she wasn't feeling well. I understood that she was COVID-19 positive. I kept quiet and didn't tell anyone anything. But couldn't stay quiet for long as her situation worsened. I confided in a friend. He was reluctant and afraid to help. So he told someone at the slum about

Radha. Soon the news spread all over the area like fire.... Yes, fire!! That fire burnt my innocent Bittu alive.

I was trying to sleep in my van when someone called up and shattered my small world. Our hut had caught fire with Radha trapped inside. Nobody came forward to help my Bittu. She must have screamed in pain but her screams were unheard by one and all. Imagining her pain and trauma makes me insane. I helplessly listened to him. I don't even remember what happened to me after that. The next morning I woke up on the hospital bed. I had passed out after the phone call. For a second I thought it was a horrifying nightmare and looked for my phone to call Bittu. But Bittu was gone never to answer my phone call.

The incident made me numb and even more mechanical. I stopped drinking because now those dead bodies didn't scare me. I tried searching for my Bittu in those black polythene bags.

Tonight when I was carrying bodies from the mortuary to my van as usual. I felt something strange. My hand was on the chest of one of the bodies. I could feel something ticking slowly... insignificantly slow. It was a heart beating! I wanted to stop and take him to the hospital but something in me didn't let me do that. I placed it with the other bodies and started the ignition of my van. My mind could now hear that heart beating loudly behind the thin tin partition. But I continued driving the van. As I reached the crematorium, I unloaded the bodies nine dead and one still living. My mind and heart both in sync, burn it alive like they burnt Bittu. And I followed my heart and mind...

SEVEN
COURAGE

The year 2030

Interviewer:

Dear Viewers, today we are here to tell you a success story... A story of a young doctor who scaled heights of success and achievements at a considerably young age. Her story of affluence and fortune is going to inspire a lot of aspiring doctors. Medical practitioners should be empathetic towards their patients and should be concerned about their patient's well-being. This is exactly what our National Doctors' Award recipient Dr. Sakshi Singh religiously follows. She had been awarded this prestigious award for her relentless and selfless dedication to the medical profession. Many of us know her as a renowned doctor who holds the credit for some important research. Dr. Sakshi has always been a private person and convincing her for an interview has been a herculean task. So without taking much of your time, let's start with the interview.

Dr. Sakshi, a bright student throughout, was honored with four gold medals in MBBS by the reputed Medical University of Lucknow. After completing her graduation in Medicine, Sakshi was offered a scholarship for further studies by a foreign Medical University but being a true Indian, she followed what her heart desired the most, completed her MD in Medicine in India itself, and ever since then there has been no looking back. She has been creating history in the world of Medicine Science.

Dr Sakshi, having you here is a momentous occasion for our channel. Thanks a lot for accepting our request for an interview. We all know, you have been a very private person all through. Your patients vouch for your name and your professionalism is what we all look up to. Tell us about your childhood. What sort of a girl you had been?

Dr. Sakshi:

Thanks for having me on board and gratitude for showering me with so much praise and affection. I am all that I am because of my people, my patients, and my staff. They are my pillar of strength.

Coming to your question, I had a normal childhood like any other Indian girl. My parents and my brother constituted my small world. I grew up happy and secure in a loving atmosphere. It was the most beautiful phase of my life.

Interviewer:

Who inspired you to choose the medical profession?

Dr. Sakshi:

There wasn't any inspiration as such, or maybe that's how I felt, it just went with the flow. I was an above-average student and my parents were quite proud of the fact, that I fared well in my studies. Both of us, my brother and I, were laborious and hardworking. In those days, there weren't many choices for a bright student, ironically. (Giggles with a nostalgic look in her eyes.) You were either a doctor or an engineer. And we two chose one each. My brother became an engineer and I chose to be a doctor.

Interviewer:

That's interesting and quite like all Indian families!

Who do you consider to be your biggest strength and support in this successful journey of yours?

Sakshi:

Till the time I had my family by my side, I never thought of needing support. But after them, my sister's-in-law mother and my niece have guided me through and have been my torchbearers. What the world sees is the success story and what they don't know is that it took me immense courage to come this far.

Interviewer:

(Nods in affirmation)

Tell us more about your story of courage, that has brought you to the epitome of success.

Sakshi:

(Stares blankly at the audience. Her mind churning with memories and thoughts. Should she say it all, that she has kept hidden within herself for years now? Her eyes searched for her niece Sonal and her godmother in the audience. Her searching eyes, stop at them, sitting in the front row. Their eyes met hers and they nodded in agreement with her...as if they knew everything that was going on within her at that moment. They did!)

(She clears her throat and says)

After having completed my MBBS in the year 2019, I started my internship with the medical college. It was all so good and beautiful. I was concentrating on my career and my family kept backing me. A couple of years ago, there was a new addition to our family, my brother Sahil got married to Shradha. She was the most elegant and defined girl I had ever seen or met. A dancer and musician, she was my stress buster. My mom's second daughter. By the end of 2019, my family was blessed with a charm, my niece Sonal. It was as if our happiness knew no bounds. We were happy and content in our world. But sometimes, what we think shall stay on forever, passes off in a blink of an eye. This is what happened to us.

(Sakshi takes a pause, and drinks some water to get rid of that lump in her throat.)

The year 2020, the blackest year in the history of mankind, took it all away. COVID-19 came as a wave, and with it took away the lives and smiles of millions across the world. I as an intern doctor, had taken charge at the hospital, with the number of COVID patients multiplying I was at the hospital almost 24by7. We had lost track of time. Days and nights all seemed one.... Dark.

One evening, I was given a break of 24 hours and I went home after a week. I wish I hadn't. Those 24 hours I spent at home were precious and my last memory of my happy family. Mom and Bhabhi prepared everything I loved. Bhaiya and Papa made sure I could relax to the fullest. I spent my best day with them. (Another lump there and she looks up at the ceiling, just to keep her tears in check.)

The interviewer and the audience were all spellbound.

Sakshi continued:

The next day, I went back to work. Hugging my family for the last time. While I got busy with work, the situation turned upside down at home. My parents, my bhaiya and bhabhi, all got infected with coronavirus. I got a call from my area's hospital that my family had tested positive and had been shifted to the Covid Care Centre. My niece Sonal, was handed over to her maternal grandmother. Fortunately, she was the only one who tested negative. A week passed by and I used to regularly get an update on their condition...which was worsening day by day. My mom was the first one to call it quits. Followed by my brother and Bhabhi. They both passed away on the same day. They were meant to be forever together. The last to give up was my father. And everything slipped out of my hand like sand. I couldn't do anything for them. Their cremation was done by the center itself. I feared going home, but had to. The moment I stepped in I could feel that warmth and comfort but all my people were missing.

I sat down on my father's chair and cried alone for hours. I had nothing left. I immediately got up and locked the house. I went back to my restroom at the hospital. It was all dark in front of me. I couldn't even muster enough courage to lift a glass and take a sip of water. It felt lifeless.

(This time, tears were flowing down her cheeks but she continued, mechanically)

I don't remember when I fainted. I was taken to the hospital and administered drips. But that shock was something I didn't want to get over. My mind and body were on different tracks. My mind was full of thousands of thoughts and anxiety. While physically I was numb... I didn't know what I wanted to do next. For a fraction of a second, I had the thought of committing suicide. And this thought made its way to my heart. I started looking out for ways and opportunities to end my life. I thought living was worthless. My family never went anywhere without me... Why did they leave me behind this time? Questions without any answers...

I tried to commit suicide two times but unfortunately was saved. A month passed away and I still couldn't retrieve myself from this traumatic incident. One day, all of a sudden, sitting in my bed, I remembered my little niece Sonal. A shiver ran down my spine, where must be Sonal. I thought, what if she was left behind in the house...

I called up my friend immediately and enquired about her. I was so lost in my pain that I forgot about my little girl. How could I be so careless... Thoughts loomed over when she answered my call and to my respite told me that Sonal was safe with her nani.

I was in hospital for over a month. Reason, severe acute depression. I used to cry inconsolably for days and nights. I thought to myself that I would go and visit Sonal for one last time and then sell my parents' house and save all the amount for Sonal's future. As for myself, I had lost my zeal to live. It was all over for me. I shouldn't be living.

(Sakshi looked at the interviewer, the girl was teary-eyed.)

What you think to be a success story, wouldn't have happened but for that lady sitting there with Sonal. (She pointed towards her godmother. She was Mrs. Sharma, Shradha's mother, Sonal's grandmother and Sakshi's godmother. Had she not been there, the story would have been entirely different.)

(Sakshi went up to her. Bowed down held her hand and brought her up to the stage. And made her sit on the couch.)

Sakshi further added:

I don't know what to call our bond I wasn't born out of her womb but I was reborn because of her. I lived because of her. (She smiled at the old lady.)

After recovering physically I went to meet Sonal. I was apprehensive about what if I wasn't welcomed there. What if they turned me out of the house? After all, I was the reason they lost their daughter. I nervously entered the house and pressed the bell button.

I didn't know that I was pressing the button to live again.

Auntyji, as I had always addressed her, opened the door. She was surprised to see me. Held my hands and took me inside. Before I could say anything, she hugged me tight. It was something I was unconsciously waiting for. I couldn't stop crying. But this time, crying made me feel light. I sat there with my head in her lap for hours. We didn't speak a word. But we understood each other's pain. Uncle and Aunty insisted that I should stay with them. Shradha Bhabhi was their only child. And the house was full of her pictures and vibes. I felt guilty for ruining their beautiful world.

I held Sonal in my arms and kept looking at her innocent face, trying to find my brother and Bhabhi in her tiny features. But she resembled me so much. Bhabhi was the elder sister I always secretly longed for. She was a friend, a guide, and everything to me. My brother once said that he wanted to have a daughter like me... intelligent and smart. But I told him that no she would be elegant and poised like Bhabhi. Creatively gifted, soft to the core, and strong as a woman. I turned out to be the weakest person. That evening, I told Uncle Aunty about my plans to sell the house and deposit the money for Sonal. As for me, I will go abroad to complete my further studies and never come back again....

(Sakshi looked at her Auntyji and clutched her hand tightly. She didn't want to break down.)

Auntyji handed me the keys to the house. And asked me to go there and collect all my belongings. I was petrified of entering that house again. I insisted that she should come along with me. But she convinced me to go alone.

The next morning, while unlocking the door, my eyes fell upon the fading yellow turmeric palm prints of my bhabhi. It was her first mark on that house. And for the years to come, she left her beauty in every corner of the house. I was shivering as I entered the house, it was all prim and proper. Auntyji took care of everything despite her loss. There in its usual corner was my father's chair. I used to sit in his lap and read the newspaper with him. He was very particular about the house, it wasn't just a building for him but it was his love. My mom's favorite spot was the balcony after the kitchen. She loved watching sunrise and sunsets sitting there. The kitchen still smelled of her. I could see her pleating my hair into two braids for school. She used to listen to me recite poems while doing her chores... Poems later transformed into stories of my growing up. I shared everything with her. There on the wall of Bhaiya's room was his wedding picture. Beautiful bhabhi and adorable bhai.... and me smiling behind them. Bhabhi's creative skills adorned the house with her charm. These memories were making my head spin. And I sat on the bed... thinking the impossible. How can I sell these memories and moments to anyone? I realized why Auntyji sent me home, alone. I called her up instantly and asked her to come over.

When she came, she brought Sonal along. She handed me my bundle of joy and kissed my forehead. She knew what my decision was. She only said one thing, "Let's start over again from scratch. We have outlived our greatest losses. It's time to live again now. Nothing could be worse than what we suffered. It's time to make everything good for Sonal."

(Sakshi hugged the old lady tight. While Sonal joined them on the couch. Sonal is getting trained as a Kathak dancer and pursuing her studies. She calls Sakshi, Maa, as taught to her by her nani.)

Interviewer:

(Takes a long deep breath, as if waking up from a reverie.)

What started as a tale of success and achievements concludes here as a story of courage and grit. Of hope from hopelessness... We all knew and respected Dr. Sakshi as a professional but now that we know her real story we are all full of awe and admiration for her.

EIGHT
FEAR

"India is walking home."

COVID-19, the pandemic, left the entire world shaken. The entire world population was affected. Every household... each section of society suffered at the hands of destiny. When the world was overcast with the grim shadows of the pandemic. India was also fighting this battle against the fatal virus. What began as a single patient infected soon started multiplying. The lives of billions of Indians were at stake. The death rate gained pace. Traveling was the first to be restricted. Flights were canceled. Trains and buses came to a halt. Airports, railway stations, and bus stops wore a deserted look. The next step was the government of India declaring a complete lockdown to save the people from Coronavirus. For the first time in history, life had come to a standstill. Roads and streets looked desolate. The ever-brimming markets were unpeopled. That's when a large section of India's working immigrants had another hurdle to cross. With no jobs in hands...no roof over their heads...no shelter for their families food for their children, they were left with no option but to return home. Home, a town, or a village, which some, left years ago and settled down in these fast-moving cities becoming the backbone of its working class. Some lured by the charm and glamour of these cities followed the suit of their predecessors and came to settle in the urban world that promised to fulfill their dreams, sometime back.

Many had forgotten what home was. For them, these cities have become home. They toiled in these places to make ends meet but never complained or thought about going back. Working as laborers at construction sites, driving autorickshaws, working as house helps. Doing all sorts of odd jobs to keep up with the pace of life. Their dreams of making it big may have been shattered but they had no regrets. This is how life was going on through all crusts and troughs. All of a sudden, an invisible virus turned their bare minimum life upside down. There wasn't a way out...

Had it been a story of a handful of families, it would have gone unnoticed and gradually life would have pulled back but this was the fate of countless families, living all across India. They were all left with no choice but to go back home...walking... on foot...

Tara and her two daughters also had the same fate. Tara and her husband Ramesh worked as house help in the high-rise apartments of Mumbai. Ramesh wasn't a professional electrician but worked as one. He even did some odd jobs for the high-profile residents of those apartments. They had a small family of four. Ramesh and Tara did all possible to give their daughters a reasonably good life. The girls studied in a local school and even helped their mother with the household chores. Twelve and ten respectively Radha and Rohini were two sweet little girls. Tara worked at five to six houses to earn a decent living. This is how life was going and they were happy in their small world. They belonged to a remote tribal village in Madhya Pradesh. Their ancestors had worked as bonded laborers for decades at the affluent families of the village. Ramesh didn't want the same fate for his daughters and wife, so he decided to break the chain. He along with his family came down to Mumbai. His brothers and uncles still work in the village. They have little or no land of their own to cultivate. They work on wages on other farms. This is how difficult life was in the village. Ramesh used to tell about his hardships to his daughters and was always encouraged to work hard and study hard to break free from the clutches of poverty.

Fate...luck... destiny, always has an upper hand. But is this fate or the result of mankind's doings? Covid 19 left an evil mark on all.

One evening Tara got a phone call from one of her employers, she told Tara that she need not come to work from tomorrow. The irony was man started fearing another man and can't even live alone. Coronavirus is airborne and easily transmitted from one person to another. Masks and sanitizers, along with social distancing became the new normal. People started avoiding each other to keep their families safe. These housekeepers were the first to be expelled from their homes. Multi-national companies and other collared jobs later got an option of working from home but these people had no work-from-home scene for them. No work meant no wages. No wages meant no food.

Tara got a little worried as to how would she manage her home. Later that day, all her employers informed her the same. None of them talked about the wages but...

It was all getting dark and grim. Her mind had stopped working. How will she manage without money? Leave aside her daughters' education, how is she gonna feed them....A big question mark loomed over her fate. This was not the end of her crisis but rather it was just the beginning. Ramesh, who had gone out of station to work at a wedding, came home sick. He had a high fever. When the neighbors got to know about him. They called up the BMC. A team of corona warriors came to their house. These people were fully covered from head to toe with masks, gloves, bodysuits, and face shields. Not even an inch of their body could be seen. The entire neighborhood was peeping through doors and windows, but no one dared to come out. The terror of an unseen virus was such that people were forced to give up on humanity.

An antigen test was conducted on Ramesh. And to the horror of the family, it turned out to be positive. Ramesh was immediately taken away to the Covid Centre in the ambulance.

This was the last Tara and her daughters saw Ramesh. He was admitted for a week but his condition instead of improving, deteriorated. He developed a breathing problem and succumbed to his ailment on the eighth day. During, this eternally long week Tara called the Covid Centre every day thrice. ' Your husband is improving.', was the only mechanical reply she got. On the eighth day, she called a call from the center stating that her husband had passed away. His body would be cremated with the others who died of Covid.

No other answer was given. She had questions and wanted to know what had happened to Ramesh. He was fine with just a mild fever and cold. How could he die? But with an array of questions her future, too got lost in this pandemic.

How will she disclose this to her daughters? How are they going to take it? And the biggest, what now....?

The three of them, cuddled up together the whole dreadful night. With no one to console or wipe their tears. Tara was a strong woman but all her strength was Ramesh and his support.

The next morning she called up her brother-in-law, Ramesh's elder brother Rajesh, and told him about his brother's demise. The whole family back home was shocked. Tara told him," Bhaisahab, I am planning to come back home with my daughters. We have nothing left here. The house is rented and with no earnings how will I manage alone here? I can stay there and work at the brick kiln."

Rajesh was apprehensive as he would now have three more mouths to feed. But couldn't even say no as the house belonged to all. He even well knew his wife's temperament. She was too authoritative and dominating. He agreed to Tara in a very low voice," As you think right, Choti Bahu. There is anyway no other option."

Tara was aware of the aftermath but had no choice. She tried to maintain her calm in front of her girls. However, she was broken and tired inside. She wanted to give up but had to keep running the race for her daughters. Radha and Rohini understood their mother's trauma but they were helpless. All they could do was abide by her decisions and support her.

They started winding up their little world. Everything in the house had beautiful memories attached to it. How elated the kids were when Ramesh had brought the television home. They invited all their friends to watch cartoons with them. The bicycle that Tara's madamji gave her may have been an old one but it was nothing less than a joyride for her girls.

Tara was lost in those precious moments when Radha asked her," Can we take the teddy bear along." It was her favorite piece of toy, torn and tattered yet soft and cozy.

" No dear! We will take only the essential items and nothing else.", Tara replied.

" Okay, mumma.", Radha was disappointed but didn't want to stress her mother more.

Tara, called up Mohan, Ramesh's friend to arrange three tickets for her to Indore. Her village was a few miles from there. Indore was 585 km from Mumbai. More than twenty-four hours of journey... Changing three buses and then a long drive to hired conveyance to her village.

Mohan told her," Sorry Tara but you cannot get tickets for either bus or train as all conveyance has been stopped till further announcement by the government. So no option."

Tara was taken aback.

Mohan even told her, that he along with his family had decided to walk down to their village in Gujarat. Everyone is doing the same and there is no other option left.

"Even you should start walking home.", he suggested.

Tara nodded.

Setting out on such a long journey on foot? How would her daughters walk? She was about to have a nervous breakdown.

She was stuck between the devil and the deep seas. Walking home was the devil she chose.

The next morning, she told her daughters that they would be walking to their village. The girls were astonished and startled... She hugged them tight. Instructed them, " Don't leave my hand even for a second. Don't talk to anyone. Don't take anything from anyone, no matter how desperately you need it."

The fear in her heart was well reflected in her eyes...voice and all her being. Her heart sank at the thought of any mishap. She prayed to God," Please to be our savior." And they began walking homeward holding hands. The girls were horrified and nervous.

As they reached the highway, they saw hundreds like them walking on an unending journey. It was a long way home. They had walked only a few kilometres and the girls became weary. Tara, encouraged them, " Once we reach home, all our problems would be over. Don't lose hope my darlings."

They walked the whole day and rested in the evening. They were on the border of Maharashtra and Madhya Pradesh when they were resting at night on the third day of their journey. It still seemed unending. Tara didn't even wink her eyes, she was so afraid of the world around her. Holding her daughters tight she looked at the road looking like a serpent, that was there to devour them all. The thoughts were so perturbing...

The other morning, came with a faint ray of hope. The state governments have started special buses to bring their people back. These buses were jammed with heads with no space to breathe leaving aside Covid protocols being followed. People just wanted to reach home. They were least bothered by what if they got infected.

Tara and her daughters boarded one such bus and set out on another hopeless journey...

NINE
HAPPINESS

"Mom, I can't take leave so often. It's not as easy as you think.",
Ritesh replied almost irritatingly to his mom.
" But Ritesh, the last you came was two years ago, and that too just
for a week. I so much wish to see you.", said Mom.
"Mom I will talk to you later, got to go, my boss is eyeing me. I
have an important presentation lined up. Take care. Love you.", and
Ritesh disconnected the call in a jiffy without even waiting for his
mom's reply.

Ritesh works as a software engineer for an American company.
After completing his studies, he secured a campus placement in this
top-notch company. He's been in LA for the last three years now...
Being the only child of Radhika and Raman, he is their world, and
like any other parents, they depend on him. Radhika had high hopes
for her son. She was the one who insisted that he should work
aboard. Sending her heart out in the world was a tough decision but
since she wanted the best for her son, she kept her feelings aside and
always supported Ritesh in his endeavors. Ritesh was a pampered
child but not a spoilt brat. He studied well and secured himself a job
in one of the highest-paying IT companies in the US. His mother's
joy knew no bounds.

His father Raman was the biggest strength of both Radhika and
Ritesh. However, he wasn't much in favor of Ritesh going to LA.
Though he did everything possible to help Radhika and Ritesh, both

realize their dreams. Both mother and son had lived this dream for long. Since childhood, Radhika planted this desire in her son's heart. Ritesh and his dream had grown up together.

Three years back, when Ritesh left for the US, the happiest person was his mother. She was a proud mother who could foresee her son's dreams coming true... She used to boast of Ritesh among her friends and relatives. Sometimes people even found her arrogant but she was least bothered.

Today Ritesh has achieved whatever many can't even dream of. But in this run for success, he left his parents' hopes far behind. The gap between them loomed deep and wide. He was so engrossed in his life in LA that he almost forgot about his mother waiting for him back home. He used to send them gifts and transferred dollars to his father's bank account. He even called them once on the weekend but he forgot that they needed his emotional support much more than these materialistic things. He was highly absorbed in building up a world for himself.

Radhika and Raman led a lonely life back in India. All they could do was wait for the weekend to hear and see their son on FaceTime. Sometimes when Ritesh was busy with something, even these weekend calls would become a luxury. Radhika got depressed and owing to her depression, she suffered from hypertension.

After that call, she cried profusely. Raman tried to console her but she was uncontrollable. That night, she wasn't able to sleep. The thought of never being able to see her son ever again made her dreadful.

She solemnly said to her husband," What if I die, without seeing Ritesh ever again."
"He doesn't love me anymore.", she added.
Raman consoled her," Don't think so. When I am there with you why do you have to worry about anything."
Raman made her lie in his lap and gently stroked her forehead. But Radhika kept sobbing.

The next morning, Raman thought Radhika had slept. So he quietly got up and went to prepare tea for her. He thought of calling Ritesh but dropped the idea. Ritesh had been busy with some important project so he didn't want to disturb him. While preparing tea, he switched on the television. This LED television, Ritesh had gifted them on their anniversary two years back. Brushing off his thoughts, he surfed channels. The news channels were highlighting the news of COVID-19 and that it has started spreading its wings in India too. Everyone was being advised to stay indoors, wear a mask, and use sanitizer. Raman had been following the news of coronavirus since its outbreak in China but now that it's in India and that was scary. The virus was not just here but it was gradually making its presence felt all over the world. While watching the news, he almost forgot about Radhika for a few minutes. He got worried about Ritesh. How would he manage there alone? He texted Ritesh:

" Take care of yourself, beta. Coronavirus is spreading rapidly and it's highly infectious."

Message sent. The message read...but no reply.

This disheartened Raman, and he remembered he had put tea on the gas stove. He went to see it boiling, he made two cups for themselves. He went to his room with tea. But Radhika was deep asleep.... no she was unconscious, suddenly Raman realized. He tried rubbing her palms.

Called out her name, "Radhika! Radhika! Open your eyes!"
He immediately called up the doctor. The doctor asked him to bring Radhika to the hospital. Raman told him," Doctor I am alone, so you would have to send an ambulance."

The ambulance reached there in no time. Radhika has been under the treatment of Dr Verma since the last year. Dr Verma checked her Blood pressure without any delay. Her blood pressure levels have been dangerously high. Soon Radhika was shifted to the ICU with all medical equipment and machines around her. Raman panicked. Seeing Radhika in this situation made his heart sink. His mind wandered straight to Ritesh... should he call him but he must be sleeping... He would get worried. Let Radhika's condition improve then he would call him... He sat beside Radhika, looking at her face, and holding her hand. Radhika was still unconscious. Dr Verma put her under observation for the next 48 hours. The longest 48 hours Raman had ever lived.

Ritesh had a long tiring day at work. He was in the middle of a conference call when he received Raman's text. He thought to himself," Papa is still so much concerned about me. I will call him once I get done with this call." The call that lasted two hours was exhausting. He forgot to call his father back home. He went into a deep slumber when all of a sudden he woke up to his mother's voice calling his name. He was sweating when he realized that it was just a reverie. But his heart was not at peace... He looked at the time, it was 2:00 AM there. He picked up his phone and without any second thoughts called up Radhika. His mother didn't answer his call...that has never happened in these three years. He got panicked. He dialed her number again. This time too his call wasn't answered. With shivering hands and all sorts of negative thoughts, he called up his father.

Raman answered his call, he got a little relieved on hearing his father's voice. But immediately realized the tension in his hello.

"Hello! Ritesh...."

" All good na, papa. Why is Mumma not picking up my phone? I tried calling her several times. Hope everything is fine. And why are you sounding so low....?"

" Your mumma is in ICU. Her blood pressure is too high.", He said all this in a robotic tone.

Ritesh knew the reason behind his mother's illness. " Don't worry Papa, mumma will be fine. I know what she wants." And he disconnected the call.

He immediately searched for tickets to India. But the tickets were all priced so high due to the increasing spread of this coronavirus. And also there was a clause at the end...

1. Passengers of all international flights entering into India from any port are required to furnish duly filled self-declaration form

(including personal particulars i.e. phone no. and address in India) and travel history, to Health Officials and Immigration officials at all ports.

2. Passengers (foreign and Indian) other than those restricted, arriving directly or indirectly from China, South Korea, Japan, Iran, Italy, Hong Kong, Macau, Vietnam, Malaysia, Indonesia, Nepal, Thailand, Singapore, and Taiwan must undergo medical screening at the port of entry.

3. Incoming travelers, including Indian nationals, are advised to avoid non-essential travel and are informed that they can be quarantined for a minimum of 14 days on their arrival in India.

Ritesh booked his ticket to Delhi for the next day. He called up his father again and told him about his coming to India. He even told him about the protocol that he would have to follow and about 14 days of quarantine. Raman was happy to hear about his homecoming but also worried about the infectious disease. Though he didn't say anything to Ritesh. He knew Ritesh was mature enough to understand the situation and would take all due precautions and follow the protocol.

Back in LA, Ritesh packed up his suitcase. Called up his boss to inform him about his going back to India. His boss advised him to take all mandatory precautions. He even informed his friends. His flight was scheduled for 1:00 AM the next morning. But owing to this havoc, he had to reach the airport hours before his flight. Long restless journey awaited him. However, he was fortunate enough to get a direct flight. But then the long quarantine period of 14 days was scary.

After a long and unending journey, Ritesh finally landed at New Delhi airport. But from here the real ordeal begins... Not an ordeal but it was a necessary protocol that had to be followed. With the entire world being affected by the pandemic everyone had to take due precautions.

Ritesh had to go through an RTPCR and then he would be quarantined in a hotel for the next fortnight. He called up his father.

"Hello, papa... I have just arrived. How is ma doing?"

"She is still unconscious... It's been three days. Doctors are trying their best. But she is not responding to medications, God knows what will happen!", Raman answered.

"You take care and follow the protocol. ", He added.

"Papa can I talk to Maa, just for a minute...", He hesitantly said.

"But she is unconscious... How will you talk..."

"Just put the phone on speaker mode and I will talk to her", he interrupted his father.

Raman quietly followed his son's instructions. He put the phone on speaker mode and caressed Radhika's forehead gently.

"Mom! I know you are upset because of me. I got so engrossed in work and life that almost forgot that you were waiting for me. But believe me, not even for a minute were you and Papa out of my thoughts. I have never said this before to you or Papa, but I love you both immensely and you people are my world. Please get well soon. And I will see you in a few days. Just get well and go home. You will find your Ritu around you soon. ", Ritesh spoke to his mom waiting for her to respond.

Miracles are what life is all about. And these miracles keep us going but what a child's voice can do to a mother, is no miracle. It's sheer love... unconditional and pure.

For the first time in the last three days, Radhika responded to the treatment. Her fingers moved and tears rolled down the sides of her eyes. Raman was thrilled to see her. He rushed to call the doctor.

The doctor was surprised to see this immediate response. He told Raman that it was a positive sign and now she would recover soon. Radhika started responding to the treatment well now and in two days, she was shifted to a private ward.

One evening, Dr Verma advised Raman to take Radhika home as the patients of COVID-19 are increasing in the hospital. It would be better if they follow the rest of the treatment from home. The disease is highly contagious and unpredictable too. Raman agreed and the next morning they went back home.

On the other hand, Ritesh was counting his quarantine days. He spends most of his time working from the hotel room. And not missed a single day without calling his mom. A life confined to the periphery of four walls seemed so meaningless. He could now imagine what his parents must have gone through all these years confined within the boundaries of his wait....while he flew high above in the sky aiming for higher dimensions. All these thoughts and how to bridge this gap kept him awake and lost. He had to decide something that would be feasible for all three of them.

Back home, Radhika was elated. Her happiness and her son would soon be with her. The world may be submerged in deep crisis but her world was full of hope and happiness. She was least bothered by what was going around the globe, all she knew was that her son would be home...

She started devoting all her time to preparations for Ritesh's homecoming. Raman was equally thrilled and excited but he acted calm and composed. Somewhere in his heart, he even feared what would happen once Ritesh had to go back. Keeping aside his apprehensions, he too engaged himself in helping Radhika. He let Radhika enjoy her newly found bliss. However, he even took care of her health, with medications on time and proper rest in between her excitements.

Finally, it was the eve of their last day of waiting. Radhika and Raman felt restless and impatient. That night when Ritesh called them up, all of them had tears in their eyes. Their long wait would finally be over. He said to his parents, "Maa and Papa, I have decided something."

"What!", They asked almost unanimously and a bit nervously.

"I am not going back to Los Angeles. This pandemic is anyway going to change the entire world scenario. And it's not coming to an end anytime soon. I have spoken to my boss and he suggested I opt for work from home right now. The IT sector can easily manage work from home. So for now I shall be working from home and later on change base from America to India. The crisis the world is going through has made me realize that I am nobody without you both. And money will never cover up for your love. So your son is finally back with you and shall always be with you."

"But, Ritesh your dreams...", Raman said.

"I have lived that glamorous life and in the end have understood that dreams can be fulfilled anywhere, all one has to do is put in the effort and have a will.", Ritesh smiled.

The next morning, was the most beautiful one. No festivals had ever felt so bright. The gloom outside couldn't hamper their joy. For the world, the pandemic may have caused havoc but for them, it brought their son home.